Sisters
Are for Making Sand Castles

BY **HARRIET ZIEFERT** • ILLUSTRATED BY **CHRIS DEMAREST**

PUFFIN BOOKS

You can go down the slide with a sister.

A sister can lick one of the beaters . . .

You can build a city with a sister.

You can watch movies with a sister.

You can chase a sister.

A sister can chase you.

You can scare a sister.

Sisters keep you company
in the back of the car.

If your sister has a boo-boo,
you can kiss it and make it better.

A sister may help you clean up your toys.

You can pretend with a sister.

You can have a pillow fight
with a sister.

You can share a fortune cookie
with a sister.

It's nice to snuggle with a sister.